For Maggie, my masterpiece

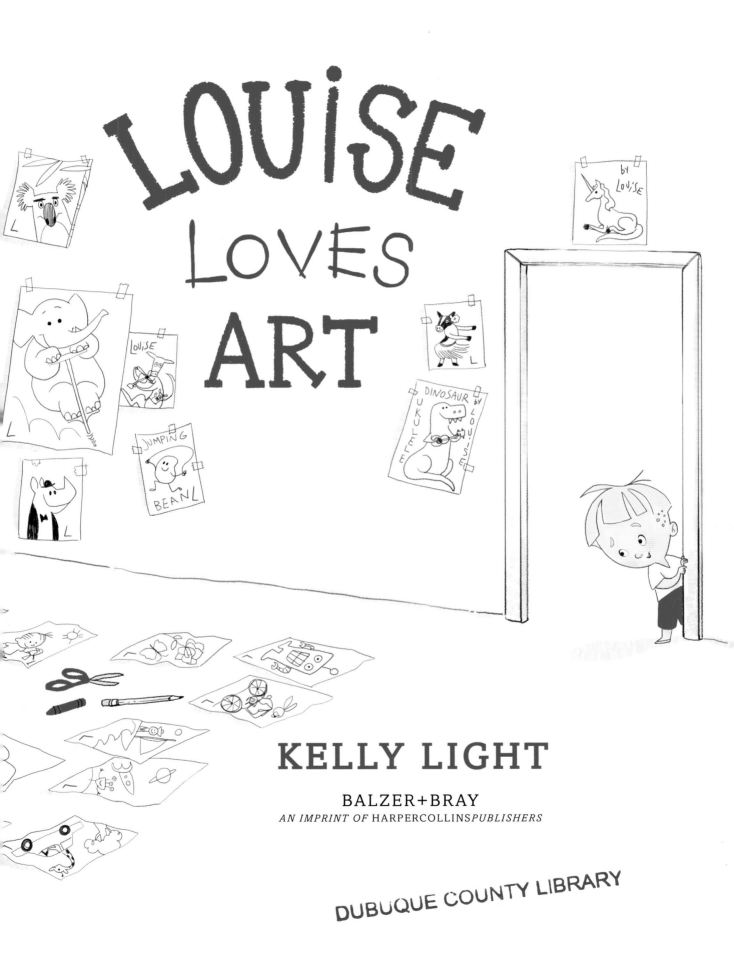

LOUISE LOVES ART

KELLY LIGHT

BALZER+BRAY
AN IMPRINT OF HARPERCOLLINS*PUBLISHERS*

I love art!
It's my imagination on the outside.

So little time, so much to draw.
One of these drawings will be my masterpiece—
the greatest drawing I have ever done!

To be a great artist, you have to notice everything.

Every line . . .

every curve . . .

Wait—hold that pose! I will capture your cat-ness!

I've done it.
So fierce! So feline! So fantastic . . .
a masterpiece!

Louise?

Not now, Art. I have to get ready for my show.

PORTRAIT OF A YOUNG ARTISTE

I have to hang each picture just so. . . .

LOUISE

Louise?

It's my pièce de résistance!
I know the perfect spot for it.

The Gallery du Fridge!

LOUISE!

AHHH!

ART!

How could you?

It's my drawing . . .

my masterpiece!

Sorry.

Oh, Art. I love it.

It's your masterpiece.
And I know the perfect spot for it.

Voilà!

Balzer + Bray is an imprint of HarperCollins Publishers.

Louise Loves Art
Copyright © 2014 by Kelly Light
For information address HarperCollins Children's Books, a division of HarperCollins
Publishers, 195 Broadway, New York, NY 10007.
www.harpercollinschildrens.com
For exclusive information on your favorite authors and artists,
visit www.authortracker.com.

Library of Congress Cataloging-in-Publication Data
Light, Kelly, date, author, illustrator.
Louise loves art / Kelly Light. — First edition.
pages cm
Summary: After drawing a picture of her cat, a
young girl searches for the perfect place to hang her masterpiece.
ISBN 978-0-06-224817-6 (hardcover)
[1. Drawing—Fiction. 2. Art—Fiction.] I. Title.
PZ7.L6253 Lo 2014   2013043069
[E]—dc23   CIP
                                                                                            AC

The artist used many black Prismacolor pencils
and Photoshop to create the illustrations for this book.
Typography by Alison Donalty
14 15 16 17 18   SCP   10 9 8 7 6 5 4 3 2 1
❖ First Edition